DATE DUE	
DEC 1 1 2007		
APR 2 3 2008		

Mouse Went Out to Get a Snack

Lyn Rossiter McFarland

Pictures by **Jim McFarland**

Farrar Straus Giroux
New York

To Tier, George, and Gracie—
rodents we have known

Text copyright © 2005 by Lyn Rossiter McFarland
Illustrations copyright © 2005 by Jim McFarland
All rights reserved
Distributed in Canada by Douglas & McIntyre
Publishing Group
Color separations by Prime Digital Media
Printed and bound in the United States of America
by Phoenix Color Corporation
Designed by Barbara Grzeslo
First edition, 2005
10 9 8 7 6 5 4 3

www.fsgkidsbooks.com

Library of Congress Cataloging-in-Publication Data
McFarland, Lyn Rossiter.
    Mouse went out to get a snack / Lyn Rossiter
McFarland ; pictures by Jim McFarland.— 1st ed.
       p.   cm.
    Summary: A hungry mouse finds a tableful of
delectable morsels in quantities which illustrate
counting from one to ten.
    ISBN-13: 978-0-374-37672-7
    ISBN-10: 0-374-37672-7
    [1. Mice—Fiction. 2. Food—Fiction.
3. Counting.] I. McFarland, Jim, 1935– ill.
II. Title.

PZ7.M4784614Mo 2005
[E]—dc22
                                    2004040360

Mouse went out
to get a snack.

Something like
a piece of cheese.

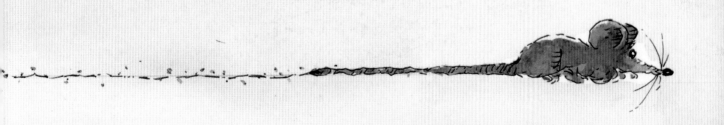

Down the hall,

around the bend.

Stop to look left and right.

**Keep an
eye out for
the cat.**

Tiptoe up the table leg.

WOW!

Yum.

Flex those muscles.

Crack those knuckles.

**First,
the big plate
over the side.**

Then . . .

1 piece of cheese

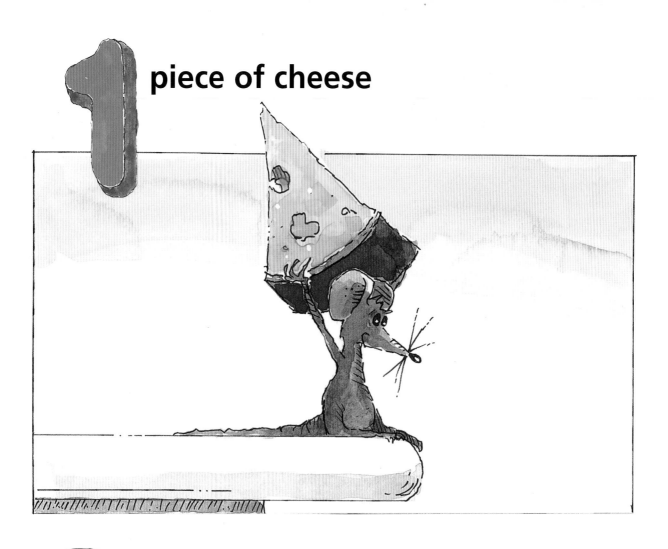

2 plump plums

3 baby carrots

4 fried chicken legs

5 ears of corn

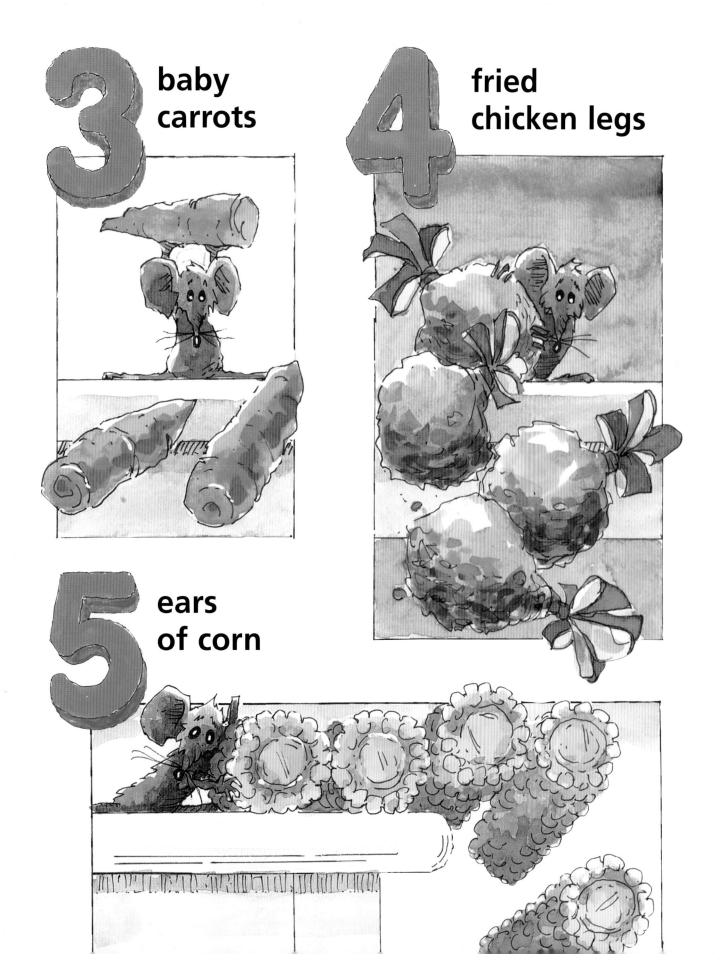

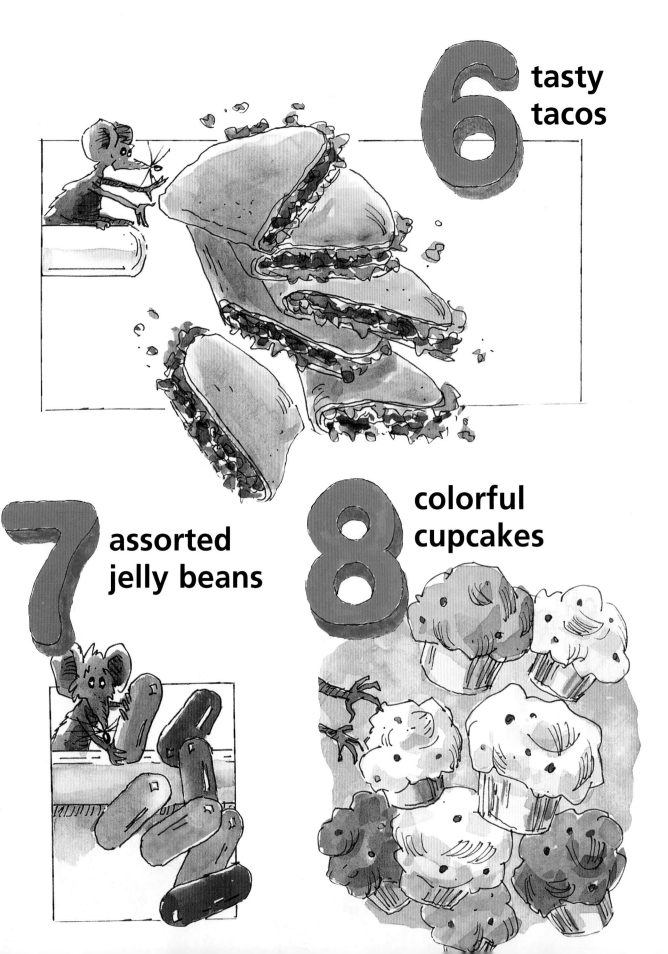

6 tasty tacos

7 assorted jelly beans

8 colorful cupcakes

9 jolly gingerbread men

10 slices of chocolate cake

PHEW!

Tiptoe down
the table leg.

Flex those muscles.

Crack those knuckles.

Pick up the plate . . .

UH

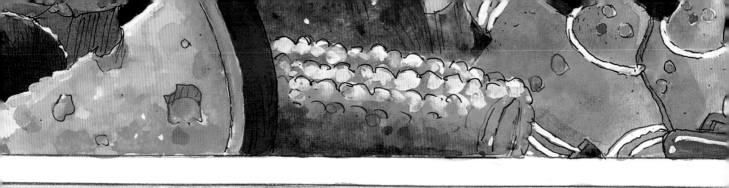

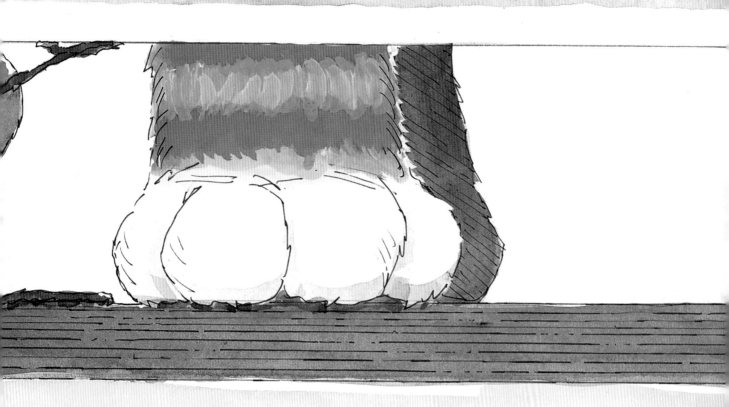

OH!

Time to go.

Through the kitchen,

around the bend,   down the hall . . .

. . . to his hole.

Too small!

Up flew . . .

and 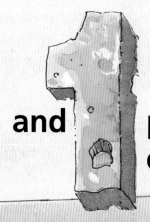 piece of cheese.

Flat cat!

Happy
mouse!